KT-394-398

Contents

1 Other Friends

'What will I wear?' I groaned as I stared into my bedroom wardrobe at a handful of neatly pressed clothes. A wall mirror across the room reflected the image of a tall slim girl with straight brown hair tied back in a loose plait, wearing a blue and red Nike warm-up suit. 'I bet Kelly will be wearing something new like the Tommy Hilfilger jumper she got last week to match her Nike Air Max runners.'

At least I was beginning to learn the names of some of the fashion labels even though I still couldn't afford to buy them. Why couldn't our family be rich like the Lynches instead of poor farmers? Dad told me once that our farm was classed as 'disadvantaged' because the land was so full of stones. Well, guess what? I feel disadvantaged when it comes to clothes – or lack of them.

My name is Clare Fox. I'm twelve years old and I live on a farm in County Galway with my mother and father and younger brother Sam. I love ponies more than anything and I was lucky enough to get the loan of one to ride at last summer's shows. His name is Timber Twig, nicknamed Piggy for short because of his dun colour and huge appetite. We ended the season by winning the Working Hunter Champion-ship at Ballinasloe Show in October. Kelly Lynch, the girl who lives in a mansion-style house in the field beside us, had a party in her dad's seafood restaurant, The Lobster Pot, in Galway to celebrate. She invited me along with a friend of mine, Maggie O'Connor, and Nick Moran, the really nice boy who helped me train Piggy for the competition. We all had a great night stuffing ourselves on jumbo prawns done in a super sauce and wild rice. Then Kelly insisted we have the house speciality, the famous chocolate mousse cake, for dessert. It was all the more fun because Kelly's friend, Brenda Fahy, was missing from the guest list. Brenda is a sort of pain the way she hangs on every word Kelly says and does, if you know what I mean.

Kelly has become one of my best friends. She loves to ride and owns a brilliant thoroughbred pony named Moonstepper. He was a bit giddy on the day of the Championship so she was only placed fourth. He's a lot better now that she has changed his feed to an oat-free pony ration.

I glanced at the small digital clock radio on the press beside my bed. The luminous red numbers glared up at me.

5.45? 5:45! 'I'm supposed to be at Kelly's at six,' I shrieked.

I started frantically pulling clothes off the hangers like I'd seen Scarlett O'Hara do in *Gone with the Wind*. Nothing looked right. My jeans were straight-legged instead of flared, my corduroys were worn at the knees, and my tops could have come from a different century. How could I be trendy wearing my cousin's hand-me-downs?

'Mom!' I bellowed, grabbing a pair of beige combats and a black polo-neck jumper that I had only minutes ago discarded on the bed. 'Where are you? I'm going to be late.' I raced out of my room to the top of the back stairs.

'What's the hurry, Cinderella?'

An impish voice calling up the stairs stopped me in my tracks. I looked down and saw a freckled-face redhead smiling up at me.

'Mags!' I sputtered.

Maggie O'Connor has been my best friend ever since I can remember. She lives on a farm across the road and we spend so much time together that our parents often joke we live in each other's pockets.

She rides too, on her brother's pony Rambo, but they don't rate in serious competition.

'What's up?' I tried to sound casual, praying at the same time that she wasn't planning to stay.

'Ye must be jokin'.' She blinked her bright blue eyes, placing her hand on well-padded hips that were encased in a lime-green warm-up suit. 'Do ye think I'd pass up an invite to eat here?'

'Oh, Mags,' I cried, 'I totally forgot. I have to go somewhere. But you can stay to tea here. I'm sure it will be okay.'

Maggie's usually cheerful face clouded over. 'Ye're goin' to Kelly's, aren't ye?' She sounded sad, but before I had time to say anything she turned and went back downstairs.

'What's worrying her?' I thought irritably. 'She knows she's my best friend. But she can't stop me having other friends.'

'Clare,' I heard Mom call from the kitchen, 'what's going on?'

I went down the stairs to the kitchen, combats and jumper in hand.

The room was warm from the heat of the Aga range. Mom was kneading dough on a floured board beside the sink, while Dad was sitting at the big wooden table having tea with John Moran. John was a family friend as well as the vet who looked after all the animals on the farm. He was the one who found the right medicine to cure Piggy of his cough before the Working Hunter Championship.

'Mom,' I said, 'do you think my combats look

okay with this polo neck? I can't wear this warm-up suit again – the Lynches will think I live in it. I'm supposed to be there at six.'

I looked up at the antique kitchen clock which hung above an old armchair, now occupied by our Jack Russell terrier Tiny; it read 5.55. Mom was now cutting out rounds of dough with the rim of a water glass and putting them on a greased baking sheet.

'Off to make the family fortune, are you?' John teased with a smile and a wink. Most of the time I enjoyed his sense of humour and silly jokes but today I was just not in the mood.

'Oh, please,' I snapped, still holding up the clothes for Mom's approval.

'What about Maggie?' she asked. 'I thought she was staying for tea?'

I watched as she opened the oven door and slid the tray of scones on to a middle rack.

'It was a mix-up. She forgot I told her I had other plans,' I said. But I could tell from the expression on her face that she wasn't convinced. She closed the oven door and faced me.

'Is anything wrong between you and Maggie?' she began. 'I can't help noticing that lately you've been ignoring her completely.'

'Mom, can this wait?' I answered hurriedly, tapping one foot impatiently against the tiled floor. 'I'm going to be late… Now, what do you think of this outfit?'

'Have you forgotten the mean things Kelly did to you last summer?' Mom was untying her apron strings. It wasn't really a question. 'I just don't want to see you in tears again.'

'Surely that's all over now,' Dad piped in. 'And, who knows, it might just be the ticket you need to buy that duck-pond field.'

'Nora,' John joked, 'are you getting into property? Wonders will never cease!'

'Well, it seems to me that that is the only logical solution after the big hassle Con Lynch caused us last summer. Padlocking the gates so that we couldn't use the right of way to our grazing fields!' Mom gave a wry smile. 'If we could gather together enough money to convince the bank to give us a loan, I would approach Mr Lynch with a bid. I know I won't rest easy until we own that field.'

'Oh, never mind me,' I said disgustedly. 'I'll wear what I have on and look like I'm straight out of the Dark Ages.' I thought to myself that one outfit was as bad as the other. 'I'll get a lift back with Vera around eight. Okay?'

Vera Lane was the Lynches' housekeeper. She lived in the village of Athenry and passed by our house twice a day. She often gave me a lift home in the evening from Kelly's house.

'Go on then if they're expecting you. But when you get home you need to phone Maggie and apologise. Ask her over tomorrow for supper.' Mom still sounded annoyed.

I grunted some sort of reply and ran out through the back door without saying good-bye. It was almost dark. The cool November air felt good on my flushed face as I ran across the paved yard. Rex, our black and white sheep-dog who had been snoozing in the stable, rose to his feet and wagged his tail excitedly when he saw me coming.

'Stay, Rex,' I yelled as I raced past him and down between the cow shed and hay barn to the small field that adjoined the Lynches' large back garden.

'Why can't Mom let me live my own life?' I muttered, as I scrambled over the stone boundary wall and headed up the manicured lawn to the brightly lit house. 'Am I to be stuck with Maggie for the rest of my life?'

2 A Stopgap

I ran up the tarred drive that led to the Lynches'
stable area and the rear entrance to their enormous
house. My runners made a scooping sound as they
hit the stone chippings of the entrance drive on my
race around to the front. Imagine having two
driveways; one for deliveries, the other for family and
friends. An old BMW was parked next to the Lynches'
silver Mercedes.

I remembered back to last summer when Maggie
and I first walked over to the 'mansion' to deliver a
letter to Kelly. We were terrified that we would be
met by a vicious rottweiler; instead of which we were
greeted by the nice Vera Lane. I pressed the doorbell
and took several gulps of air while I waited for her to
open the door. I was still breathless from my sprint
over.

'Clare, darling,' gushed a voice as the door opened
and I was smothered in a cloud of strong perfume.
'What a wonderful surprise! Do come in and meet
our "special" guests.'

I found myself standing face to face with Kelly's
mother. Marion Lynch, who had never bothered to
say more than a word or two to me in the past, was
now inviting me in to meet her 'special' guests. I was
flabbergasted.

'Thanks, Mrs Lynch,' I managed to say as I

followed her through the circular front hall to a set of French doors that led into a large sitting-room. Mrs Lynch was what clothes designers would call a perfect size 10. She was dressed in a black lounge suit which was a striking contrast to her ultra-blonde highly styled hair. She wore dark eyeliner and red lipstick that framed a set of dazzling white teeth that must have cost her a fortune in dentist's bills.

'Your carpet is lovely,' I said nervously, as we walked through the hall. 'Is it Chinese?' I'd seen an ad for Chinese carpets from some posh Galway store.

Marion Lynch looked back at me pityingly. 'Persian, antique Persian. An antique Persian rug,' she laughed, shaking her head so that all the gold jewellery she wore on her fingers, wrists, and ears twinkled like a set of Christmas lights. As I followed her into the sitting-room I made a mental note to ask Mom about carpets and rugs, especially at the top end.

'Kelly, sweetheart,' Mrs Lynch cooed. 'Your riding friend is here... Now, let me introduce you to our friends.' She batted her heavily blackened eyelashes and locked her arm around mine as we walked through the room.

Kelly was settled in a huge armchair, talking to a boy about her own age who was perched on the arm of a matching overstuffed chair. Sitting across from them a girl who looked like him. A woman dressed in the kind of tweeds you'd see in top riding outfitters – their mother? – reclined in another armchair. A silver tray holding several bottles and glasses, attended by a neat little maid, was set up on a table behind the couch, while a blazing fire crackled in a marble fireplace in the background. The combination of rich colours, another antique rug, gleaming mahogany and brocaded upholstery screamed of interior decorators and lots of money.

'Eleanor,' Mrs Lynch purred as she manoeuvred me to a spot directly in front of the older guest. 'This is Clare, Kelly's riding friend. She's the one I told you all about, who won the Working Hunter Championship at Ballinasloe last month. She's going to Dublin next summer to win her class at the RDS.'

'I guess,' I mumbled, feeling my face flush with embarrassment at the fulsome introduction. It made me sound like Eddie Macken.

I was also embarrassed by my totally inappropriate clothes. Imagine wearing a track-suit to a drinks party!

And to think of all the time I'd spent at home trying to put together an outfit. I could have strangled Kelly in her cashmere twin-set, calf-length skirt and leather pumps.

'Hello, I'm Eleanor Blake,' the woman said in a voice that sounded like her mouth was stuffed with marbles. As she extended a hand for me to shake I detected the distinct odour of mothballs coming from her suit. She was tall and angular and reminded me of Max's sister in the film *Rebecca* I'd seen lately on telly. The only thing that was missing was the hat with a feather in it.

'And these are my children, Charlotte and

Charles.' The boy and girl – Charlotte tall and dark like her mother; Charles stocky with a mop of sandy fair hair – struggled to their feet.

'Mummy,' Charlotte yawned, ignoring me completely, 'what time does the cross-country start tomorrow? I still need to pick up my hacking jacket from the cleaners.' She, too, was wearing a twin-set, long skirt and leather shoes.

'Tut! Tut!' Charles mocked, looking at me with a big grin. 'Terrible to have to be a fashion plate. Hi, I'm Charles Blake. Nice to meet you.' He took his hands out of the pockets of his baggy corduroy trousers and offered me one. I liked him immediately. At least he was friendly.

'The cross-country?' Mrs Blake wrinkled her brow in an effort to remember. 'I think it's two o'clock.

Yes, definitely two o'clock… Charlotte and Charles,' she explained to me, 'are riding in a pony club final. It's sponsored by Lord and Lady Laverton. We've all been invited back to the castle afterwards for afternoon tea.' She turned to Mrs Lynch. 'I find the weekends packed, especially now that the two are weekly boarders at Mount Inver.'

'Another G & T?' asked Mrs Lynch.

'Oh, please.' Mrs Blake settled back in her chair. 'Now do tell us about this competition you rang me about.'

I felt like a fish out of water with all the talk about boarding-schools, pony clubs, castles and afternoon tea, but I was determined not to let it show. I sat on a chair near Kelly sipping my Coke, trying to look interested in the conversation.

'It's called the Team Hunt Chase.' Mrs Lynch sounded as if she'd been around horses all of her life. 'Con has already booked an instructor to come here on Saturday mornings to coach the four members of the team. Of course we'll take care of his costs as well as the entry fee for the competition.'

'And the prize?' Mrs Blake asked.

'Each of the winning team members will receive a crystal rose bowl – I have a spot already picked out for Kelly's in my new china cabinet.' Mrs Lynch clasped her hands so that her multi-caret diamond ring exploded into sparks.

'And the prize money?' Mrs Blake took a long sip from her drink.

'Oh, I'm sure there's a cash prize as well. I'll check

with Con tonight.' She nodded to the maid who took Mrs Blake's glass and refilled it.

'Sounds great,' said Mrs Blake. 'I'm sure the children will get on splendidly together. You must all come over to the house one of these days and have supper with us.'

'We'd love to,' said Mrs Lynch, trying not to sound over-eager.

I was beginning to get the picture – and with no thanks to Kelly who had her eyes glued to Charles. I was to be the fourth member of the team.

I knew I was a stopgap but I didn't care. It was a dream come true.

Maybe in time I'd get to like Mrs Lynch. Not to mention 'the gorilla', as Maggie had christened her husband, Con Lynch.

3 Over the Moon

'Can I go?' I repeated. 'This is the best thing that has ever happened to me.'

I slumped into the armchair next to the Aga in the kitchen, sending Tiny scampering off to find a new spot to sleep. Mom was sitting at the table flipping through a few old stallion directories. The kitchen clock stood at ten to six. Dad would be in shortly to watch the Six O'Clock News on telly.

It had been exactly twenty-four hours since my visit to the Lynches. Twenty-two since I had dashed in to announce to Mom and Dad (luckily John had gone home), 'Can you believe it? Kelly wants me to be on her team for the Team Hunt Chase. Kelly Lynch, Charlotte Blake, Charles Blake, and Clare Fox! It will be class!'

And I still hadn't got an answer.

I glanced over at Mom who was studying a page from one of the directories. People often remark how much we look alike because we are both tall and lanky and have the same colour hair. But Mom's hair is short and curly while mine is long and straight.

'Mom, what are you doing?' I asked irritably as I got to my feet and walked over to the table. 'Kelly is going to phone me at seven to see if you'll let me be on the team, so will you please say yes?'

'Ballinrobe Boy,' Mom whispered, moving her

finger down the page. 'Just give me a second...'

Ballinrobe Boy? What was she on about?

'Mom,' I said raising my voice, 'you're not making any sense and I need an answer.'

'Okay, okay,' she said distractedly, closing the directory and gathering up the others and putting them all on the top of the fridge. Then she filled the kettle and placed it on the range.

'Dad will be in any minute and I haven't made the tea,' she said opening the fridge. I watched as she took out slices of the meat we had had for our dinner earlier that day and placed it on the table.

'Mom,' I asked, as I picked up a small piece of meat from the plate and popped it into my mouth, 'what's with all the stallion directories? You never used to read them.'

'Oh, those,' she said. 'I have an idea as to how we can raise enough money to bid Mr Lynch for the duck-pond field. That is, of course, if he will agree to sell it. I think maybe he will.'

'How?' I asked. Maybe if I listened to her for five minutes, she'd listen to what I was trying to say about the team.

'If I can prove that my mare, River Run, is a pure Irish Draught, I'll be able to enter her in all the Irish Draught mare classes next summer. The prize money can be very good, depending on the shows you enter. And there are some championships as well that pay up to £1,000 for first place. I know she can win – if I can only get the Irish Draught Society to register her.'

I shrugged. I'd only vaguely heard of draught horses. Big brutes that pulled carts.

'Do you remember when your dad and I did the charity cross-country ride last spring?' Mom asked, cutting soda bread into thick slices.

'Sure.'

'Well, during one of the checks, a French woman, who owns a horse farm in Loughrea and only shows the best sort of mares, approached me and asked if River Run was registered. I said I didn't know. She went on to say that if she was a full RID – Registered Irish Draught – she would be worth thousands of pounds as a top-class show mare.'

'How's the craic?' a voice sounded from the other side of the room and Maggie waltzed into the kitchen wearing a colourful pair of overalls that made her look like she had swallowed a balloon. I'd forgotten Mom had insisted I ask her for tea – just to make up for the night before.

'Hi, Mags,' Mom and I answered in unison, though my 'hi' was rather hollow. Why couldn't she have waited for another ten minutes. I wanted to be alone with Mom; I needed an answer about the team. I looked pleadingly at her.

'What's up?' asked Maggie suspiciously, tip-toeing backwards towards the door. She was as sharp as two buttons. 'Will ye go easy, Mrs F? Clare didn't do it, and if she did, she didn't mean to.' She burst out in a peal of laughter. I wasn't amused.

'Anything to eat, I'm starving!' Another voice came from the top of the back stairs. Sam, my ten-

year-old brother, blew into the kitchen in his stocking feet and skidded across the tiled floor.

'Sam, don't interrupt,' I snapped. 'I need to talk to Mom... Well, Mom, do I have your permission?' I whispered, glancing over at Maggie to see if she had heard me. I could tell by her expression that she probably had.

'I'll ask your dad when he comes in... Now let's get this table set. Sam, tea will be ready in a minute so go wash your hands and face.'

'Clare, do ye want to sleep over?' Maggie asked as she put five plates around the table. 'Ma let me rent a video and says we can camp out in the front room.'

'Tea ready?'

Dad's voice and appearance at the back door saved

me from having to respond. I was in no mood for a sleep-over at the O'Connors.

Dad padded into the kitchen in his stocking feet, having left his wellies in the back hall. He switched on the portable telly that was on a shelf next to the old wooden dresser.

'How are my girls?' he smiled at all of us as he took a seat.

'Include me out,' shouted Sam, racing across the floor.

Dad was dressed in jeans and a woolly jumper with bits of straw stuck to it. His dark curly hair and stocky frame made me think of a picture postcard I had seen the other day in town, of a farmer standing beside his donkey and cart at the side of a road. Farmers, it seems, never really change.

'I'm glad you're here, Tom,' Mom said. 'Kelly Lynch has asked Clare to ride Piggy in a team event. It includes practising at Lynches for the next few Saturdays. What do you think?'

'I'll go as the "chef",' Maggie blurted out. 'I saw how it's done on the telly.'

'It's called chef-d'equipe, Mags,' I corrected. 'And I'm not sure we need a manager.'

Dad took a deep breath and a slice of bread before answering. 'Clare, I don't have to remind you about all the problems the Lynches have caused us over the past six months. Between locking the duck-pond gates so that we couldn't move the cattle and sending us threatening solicitor's letters, they've been far from friendly. Still, I don't believe in dragging children into grown-up matters. It's nothing to do with you and Kelly...'

'Does that mean yes?' I cried, running over to give him a hug.

'Just be careful and mind yourself,' said Dad, squeezing my arm affectionately. 'Now, Miss O'Connor, how about you and I forming our own team? We'll call it the "Let's go to Supermac's".'

He winked at her.

4 Mr Frank

'Do you have everything?' Mom asked as she turned the jeep in the yard and headed down the main road to Athenry. It was Monday morning, the start of another school week.

'Guess so,' I muttered from the back seat, still peeved that Sam had once again won the daily sprint from the back door to the jeep and got the front seat.

'Sam,' said Mom, 'see if you can find Galway Bay FM for me. I want to hear what time the Mass for old Mrs Beirne is.'

I have to admit that even though my brother is a pain, he's a genius at anything mechanical. I watched him deftly tune to the proper station in a matter of seconds and adjust the balance on the speakers. I sat back and tried to block out the drone of the local news broadcast by letting my mind drift off. I thought about Kelly and the Blakes. I had so much to think about these days. Saturday practice at the Lynches, my new friends, and the team event looming in the distance. I hoped Piggy would behave.

St Colman's is a three-teacher primary school. Each teacher has three different classes to instruct except for the head, Miss Maher, who teaches just Fifth and Sixth. Maggie and I are in Sixth. We both love Miss

Maher; in fact, the whole school does. She is young, pretty, wears great clothes and plays basketball with us during lunch-break. What more could you want?

The class had just started. 'Good morning, boys and girls,' Miss Maher was saying as I managed to slip into my seat unnoticed at the back of the room. She was wearing a loose-fitting jumper over a long skirt and leather boots. Her dark-brown hair with a reddish tinge was cut short enough to reveal a pair of long dangling earrings that matched the colour of her jumper.

'Good morning, Miss Maher,' we all chanted back in unison as I fumbled through my school-bag searching for my pencil-case.

'A new student is joining us today, in Fifth,' Miss Maher went on. 'Her name is Kelly Lynch, and I know you will all make her feel very welcome.'

My heart did a flip-flop when I heard the name and I looked up to see Kelly grinning at me. She was standing beside Miss Maher, wearing a brand-new blue school uniform. I had been so sure she was going to boarding-school. What was she doing here?

'Kelly, is there anyone in the room that you know?' asked Miss Maher.

'Clare Fox. She lives next door to me.'

'Good,' said Miss Maher. 'And we're in luck. There's an empty seat at Clare's table.' (She didn't mention why; which was that Maggie and I had been separated the week before for too much talking during class.) 'Why don't you sit there for the next couple of weeks until you learn the routine? I'm sure

Clare will be happy to show you around and I can lend you any books until you get your own. Is that all right with you, Clare?'

'Sure, Miss Maher,' I said, smiling up at Kelly as she walked through the classroom to my table.

'Now, will both Fifth and Sixth classes open your folders and take out the poem "The Carol-Singers" by Margaret Rhodes. There are four verses. Each table will recite a stanza until everyone has had a turn. I'm looking for rhythm and proper enunciation. All right, first table, when you're ready.'

I opened up my folder and took out the printed sheet of poetry. I placed it halfway between Kelly and me. She looked at me and rolled her eyes. I shrugged my shoulders in mock sympathy. She took out her pen and sketched a funny face on the corner of the page. I did a similar one on the opposite corner. Then she drew two sets of crossed lines for a game of Xs and Os. I placed the first X, Kelly continued with an O.

'Clare, still with us?' Miss Maher's voice broke in upon our championship round. I stole a glance over at Maggie at the next table and she gave me a two-finger sign as I began to recite the second stanza:

> *I sat upright to listen,*
> *For I knew they came to tell*
> *Of all the things that happened*
> *The very first Noel.*

'Kelly, please continue,' Miss Maher prompted. I looked at Kelly and was surprised to see that her face

was pale and her fingers were trembling. I pointed to
the next stanza.

'*Upon my…*' Kelly hesitated.

'*Ceiling,*' I whispered under my breath.

'*Upon my ceiling…*' Kelly balked again. I could feel
her eyes asking me for help.

'*Flickered,*' I whispered.

'*Upon my ceiling flickered.*'

Kelly started once more but a knock on the
classroom door cut short the reading. A boy put his
head around the door.

'Miss Maher,' he said. 'You're wanted on the
phone.'

'Thank you, Sean,' she said. 'That will do for now.
Sixth class, begin taking down the problems from the
blackboard. Fifth, take out your English reader and
start reading our new story "Escape" on page ninety-
two. Kelly, here is a reader you can use for now. Be
good, everyone…and no noise.'

She left the room.

The week passed by uneventfully. Kelly and I spent
most of the school day together. We sat in the same
classroom, hung around together during breaks, and
even stood together after school waiting for our lifts
home.

Sometimes Maggie joined us, sometimes she went
off with others in the class. I could sense she didn't
like Kelly all that much but she was unfailingly
polite. I told myself she'd come around in time. We'd
be a threesome instead of a twosome.

Saturday morning arrived and I saddled up Piggy for a short ride over to the Lynches. Kelly had told me at school the day before that the team practice would start at ten o'clock sharp. I cut down through the duck-pond field, through the gate that led into the Lynches' garden and around to the back. As I approached the sand-ring I could see Kelly trotting her pony Moonstepper around in a circle. Charlotte and Charles Blake were standing next to their ponies in the centre of the ring chatting to a tall thin man. A blackboard was set up on an easel beside him.

'Mr Frank,' Kelly shouted, slowing Moonstepper down to a walk when she saw me coming. 'This is Clare, the girl I was telling you about.'

'Clare,' the man said in a deep military-style voice, 'I'm Mr Frank, your instructor. Please join the rest of the team in the arena.' He walked over and opened the gate for me.

He was wearing a beautifully tailored tweed hacking jacket, a blue-striped shirt and blue and white spotted tie, with beige breeches and a gleaming pair of black leather riding-boots. In his hands he held a hunting-cap, riding-whip, and a pair of gloves. I glanced around at the others as I rode Piggy into the ring and saw that they were also in proper riding clothes. Why hadn't I worn my navy riding-jacket instead of a nylon windbreaker? I felt totally underdressed – for the second time in just over a week.

'Will you please all line up on your ponies in front of me so that I can inspect your tack?' he directed in a commanding voice. 'It is essential for a pony to be properly bitted, bridled, and saddled. I will expect you from now on to have your tack saddle-soaped and oiled before each practice session.'

Kelly was smiling sweetly at Mr Frank. She must have known that she and her pony were perfectly turned out. She was wearing a slate-blue tweed jacket, white stock-tie, beige jodhpurs and brown boots and hat. Moonstepper's coat gleamed against his well-oiled English tack. Charlotte had a bored look on her face as she brushed imaginary bits of lint from her impeccable riding-jacket. Her grey pony chewed nervously at its bit, spotting its dappled coat with speckles of spit. He, too, was perfectly groomed, due to the obvious efforts of Mrs Blake who was standing ringside with a cloth and body-brush in her hand. Charles, wearing a riding-jacket that was several sizes too big for him over a pair of old-fashioned jodhpurs that must have belonged to his grandfather, looked relaxed and happy. So well he might have been; his clothes, though too big, shrieked high-quality tailoring. His big-boned chestnut pony was clean and properly tacked but looked half asleep as it stood lethargically at the end of the line.

I knew I was the odd one out. Well, Piggy would be groomed to within an inch of his life for future sessions. And I would just have to get a new riding-jacket. My jodhpurs, given to me by Nick as a present for winning the Championship, were fine but a new jacket was essential. I would have loved a new pair of boots but even my wildest dreams couldn't stretch that far.

'Now, then,' Mr Frank said having checked all the ponies' tack, 'before we start the lesson, I would like to review a few important points on the blackboard here.' Walking over to the easel he picked up a piece of chalk and drew a rough sketch of a figure sitting on a horse.

'You must always be in balance with your pony. Balance is determined by three straight lines. One from your shoulder to your elbow to your heel,' he said drawing that line. 'The second is from your head to your knee to your toe. The third is from the pony's mouth to your hand.' He drew these lines as he spoke, then turned to us. 'This is true for the walk, the trot, and the canter. When you jump, the lines will shift momentarily.'

He put down the piece of chalk and lightly brushed his hands. 'Now let's put all this into practice. Will you please pick up a walk and follow the black pony right-handed around the arena?'

'Very pukka sahib, isn't he?' whispered Charles to me as we got into position.

What did *that* mean? I wondered. Would I ever be able to keep up?

And I wasn't thinking of the practice ahead.

5 Testing the Water

For the first time in my life I was actually looking forward to going to school on Monday. I hadn't seen Kelly since our practice session on Saturday and I was anxious to hear what she thought of Mr Frank.

Maggie had also been away; she and her mother had taken the early train to Dublin on Saturday to see her cousin's new baby and they were getting the late train back on Sunday night.

As we pulled up before the school, I tapped Mom on the shoulder (Sam had grabbed the front seat again).

'Be sure to tell Dad not to let Piggy eat too much grass, I have him on a special fitness programme for the next few weeks. Don't forget.'

'That's the second time you've told me.' Mom sounded slightly annoyed. 'Now have a good day – and forget Piggy for an hour or two.'

I slammed the door and followed Sam up the school path.

'Clare,' I heard a voice call from the side of the school building and I turned to see Kelly beckoning me. She was wearing a very snazzy-looking navy fleece jacket over her uniform. Her school-bag was on the ground beside her.

'Hi, Kelly,' I said brightly, walking up to her. 'Thanks for Saturday. What did you think of Mr

Frank? Do you think he was kind of strict?'

But Kelly wasn't interested in Mr Frank. She said quickly, 'Clare, I need your help.' She glanced over her shoulder to see if anyone was listening.

'Sure,' I said, wondering to myself how on earth could *I* help *her?*

'Can I have your answers to the history questions?'

I couldn't believe it. She was asking me to help her to cheat. Maggie and I often did our homework together but we never copied each other's work outright.

'Well, can I?' Kelly's voice was more insistent this time.

'I guess so,' I whispered, feeling my spine tingle as I heard myself say the words. 'My history copy is in

my bag.' I pulled it out, looking around quickly to
see if anyone was watching. Luckily the coast was
clear.

'Thanks,' Kelly said as she took out her own copy
and a pen and started taking down the answers I held
out for her to see. All the time I was keeping watch
in case anyone should come around the side of the
school.

Suddenly, out of the corner of my eye, I saw
Brenda Fahy appear.

'Quick!' I hissed.

Kelly hastily handed me back my history copy and
shoved her own into her bag.

Had Brenda seen anything? She didn't give any
indication as she came up beside us. She was
smirking as she fiddled with a string of beads that she
wore around her neck. I could never figure out what
Kelly liked about her. Her small frame and dark
closely cropped hair made her look rather like an ill-
tempered pixie from one of my childhood story-
books.

Just then the bell rang and Kelly and Brenda went
around to join the queue at the door. I followed
slowly. I felt weak as a kitten. I was miserable that
Kelly wanted me to cheat and terrified that Brenda
might have guessed what we were up to. I tried to
think it was a once-off. Maybe Kelly had forgotten –
or hadn't had the chance – to do her history homework and didn't want to admit it in class. After all,
she'd only been in school a week. So I reasoned to
myself.

But the black cloud wouldn't lift.

I was relieved I didn't see her after school. I didn't purposefully avoid her but I was glad to observe, from a distance, her getting into the Lynch Mercedes. Brenda was with her.

'Where's Maggie?' asked Mom. She usually came home from school with me on Mondays – her mother worked late on that day – but she wasn't outside the gate as usual.

'I don't know,' I said, more or less truthfully. 'I didn't see her after lunch-break. Maybe she went home early.'

'Well, we can't hang around. I've got to get over to Kinvara after dinner.'

I didn't ask her why. I was thinking about Maggie. Was she still sore at me over Kelly, especially now I was spending so much time with her at school? Was there any chance she could have gone on ahead? Hardly. I'd have to wait until tomorrow to see where I stood.

'Where's Maggie?' Dad asked as we sat around the kitchen table having our dinner. We always had our main meal when we came home from school. Dad didn't care because he was around the farm anyway and Mom said it was good to have it then so Sam and I wouldn't fill up on snacks. I put down my knife and fork. Bacon and cabbage was usually my favourite dinner but somehow today it had lost its appeal.

'She's away, visiting relations in Dublin,' I lied, trying to sound normal.

Mom gave me a sharp glance. I knew I'd given the impression I'd seen Maggie at school that morning. But I could have made a mistake and just have remembered about her being away, couldn't I? Why was everyone so interested in Maggie all of a sudden? I just hoped she wouldn't turn up later.

'Anyone for a bit of a drive?' Mom asked as she cleared away the dinner plates from the table.

'Can't,' Sam answered grabbing his jacket. 'I'm going to Colm's to play hurling.'

'Where are you off to?' Dad asked.

'Kinvara – to track down a man called Mattie Stone.' She was loading up the dishwasher.

'You're what?'

'I think he may have owned the grand-dam of River Run,' explained Mom. 'And if he did, I need to know how she was bred. The Irish Draught Society said that they will only register River Run as a pure Irish Draught if I can prove that both her dam and sire, as well as her grand-dam and grand-sire were all full Irish Draught. There must be three generations of pure breeding.'

She picked up the jeep keys from the counter and headed for the back door, grabbing her anorak off one of the hooks.

'Coming, Clare?'

'No,' I mumbled. 'I've got too much homework to do.'

With a parting shot of, 'Make sure Sam is back from Colm's before dark. And gets his lessons done,' Mom was gone.

I left Dad absorbed in his newspaper and slowly climbed the back stairs to my room. I couldn't help thinking about Kelly and what she had asked me to do. All during dinner I had been wondering whether I should mention the homework episode. But I knew if I did Mom would immediately say she had been right about the Lynches. She would have wanted me to give up the team.

I went to bed early that evening. I should have exercised Piggy before it got dark but I wasn't in the mood. I lay awake for a long time. Maybe the Kelly thing wasn't such a big deal.

But where was Maggie? Had she decided to walk out on me?

6 Team Practice

It had been a strange week. Kelly had her maths homework all present and correct on Tuesday and I began to relax. Maybe she was good at maths, bad at history and reading. So, hopefully, the history cog was a one-off affair.

She was missing on Wednesday so the question of homework didn't arise on Thursday. I was half dreading an approach from her that day but she never came near me. She and Brenda seemed to be back on their old footing again. Friends? Or was she copying from Brenda? Knowing Brenda's class record, I knew that that wasn't such a bright idea.

And I was right. On Friday, Miss Maher slated the pair for some mistake so stupid that, as she pointed out, it was hard to imagine one person making it, never mind two. I wondered what Kelly would do now?

Maggie seemed as friendly as usual. But if I didn't actively seek her out at break, she'd pair off with one of the O'Brien girls. She came over to tea once – Dad met her and extended an invite – but didn't stay on. Excuse: homework. That tired old excuse.

I banished Kelly and Maggie from my mind. Mr Frank the following day was more important.

'Ladies and gentleman.' Mr Frank called for

attention from the centre of the sand-ring, tapping his riding-whip against the palm of his hand for effect. It was Saturday and the team had gathered at Lynches.

'First I want to tell you something about the Team Hunt Chase. It's a relay race over obstacles. There are four members on a team, with two teams competing at the same time over identical courses. The starter tosses a coin to decide the order of the teams, then which course you'll ride. The first team to complete the course wins the round and goes on to compete against the winner of the next round. And so on.'

'Do you have to tag the person or pony?' Charles asked.

'Neither,' said Mr Frank. 'You pass over a riding-whip to your team-mate when you change over. We will be practising that next week.'

'What if you knock a fence?' I asked, not feeling particularly confident.

'It doesn't matter as long as you manage to stay between the two flags on each fence – the red flag will be to your right, the white flag to your left.'

'What if your pony runs out or refuses?' asked Kelly.

'You'll have to turn him back and try again until you get him to jump between the two flags.'

'Who'll go first?' Charlotte asked. 'I hope not me. I get too nervous.'

Mr Frank smiled. 'Everybody gets nervous and nobody likes to go first,' he said. 'The best strategy is to let a good pony lead off, put the weakest pony second, another good pony third to make up time if need be, and the fastest pony last. Now let's talk about the type of fences you may encounter.' He turned and faced the blackboard which had a diagram of a relay course blocked out on it.

'Remember they're all knockable and none of them is over three feet in height. The first will probably be some kind of hedge, maybe followed by a pole. Then a gate and a table-like jump; this is where you ask your pony to gallop on. There will probably be a bank-type jump at the far end of the course, and you'll need to slow down for it in order to make the turn. Then a drop off the bank, followed by some sort of chute to turn through. Then a final kick for home over a couple of more straight-forward fences. We'll walk the course on the day naturally but for now I have made up a sequence of three fences in the sand-ring to practise on.'

This was it. My heart thumped.

'The black pony will pick up a collected trot, going left-handed around the ring. At the top of the arena he will change direction and pick up a canter. Maintaining this pace he will jump the hedge, followed by the gate, followed by the spread. The grey pony will follow ten lengths behind, then the dun, then the chestnut. Keep a steady pace and an even distance. When you're ready, please begin.'

Mr Frank expected discipline, control, and results. Surprisingly, we mostly rose to his challenge. He never chatted or called us by our individual names.

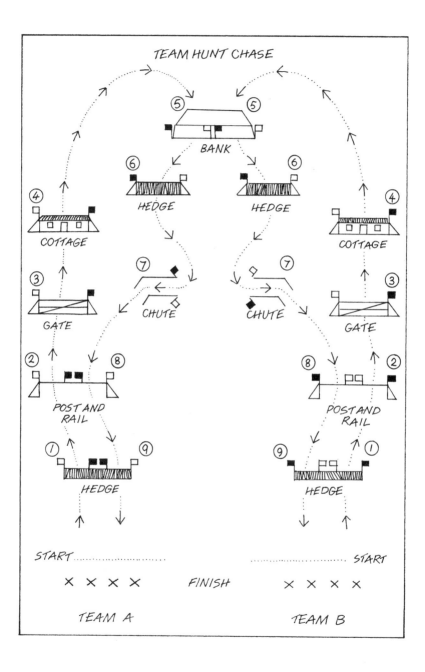

Instead he referred to the colour of the pony we rode. Kelly was always in the lead on Moonstepper. She showed natural balance and rhythm and set a steady pace for all of us to follow. Charlotte went second on Grey Mist; her pony was apt to rush at his fences but was held in check between Moonstepper and Piggy. I went third on Piggy, while Charles brought up the rear on his chestnut pony. Hobo was big and lazy and tended to slow down the pace going into a fence if given half a chance. Mr Frank thought that having three ponies moving steadily in front of him might help to increase his momentum. And it seemed to be working.

By the time we had completed five different rounds, plus the initial warm-up exercises and flatwork, I could tell from the look on everyone's face that we were all ready to call it a day.

'Does Sergeant Frank know this is supposed to be fun?' Charles whispered to me as we waited for Kelly and Charlotte to start the next round.

The fact that Charles and I were the last in the line-up inevitably meant we were standing around together at times. Unlike Charlotte, who kept very much to herself, Charles was friendly and would pull up beside me, bubbling away about anything and everything. Once or twice I saw Kelly looking back at us when Mr Frank was focusing on Charlotte and it made me feel uncomfortable. I didn't know how well she knew Charles but, thinking back to last summer when Nick was coaching me, I knew she always wanted to be first – and favourite – with everyone.

'If he does, he's got a weird idea of fun,' I whispered back and we both giggled as Kelly set off at a trot left-handed around the ring. I could feel Piggy anticipating his turn as I waited for Charlotte to go off second.

'Easy, boy!' I patted his strong shoulder. 'You're next.' I looked back at Charles who gave me a wink as I pushed Piggy forward into a steady trot. I followed Charlotte left-handed, trying to remember everything Mr Frank had taught us, as well as keeping ten lengths behind. I could hear Charles and Hobo following me as we all crossed the ring in perfect stride.

The trouble began at the top of the arena when Kelly, instead of turning Moonstepper to the right and picking up a canter, turned him to the left. When she picked up her canter I could see she had lost her concentration. She knew she had done something wrong and was going far too fast to make a proper turn into the first fence. I instinctively checked Piggy back knowing that she was headed for disaster.

And she was. Moonstepper made a huge leap over the hedge, landing at the base of the gate. He panicked and frantically tried to jump the gate from a standstill but failed to get his back legs over the top rail. There was a terrible sound of falling rails as the gate crashed to the ground.

'Kelly,' roared a voice from outside the ring. 'What the frig do you think you're doing? Go back and take that jump again. And this time do it right.'

Charlotte, Charles, and I slowed our ponies back

to a walk and looked in the direction of the shouting. Con Lynch was outside the sand-ring pointing his finger at Kelly.

'Hold on!' Mr Frank came forward. 'You mustn't interrupt the lesson. Besides she can't jump the fence. It has to be rebuilt.'

'Interrupt!' came another roar. 'I'm paying for these frigging lessons and the first thing I see when I come out is Kelly acting like she's never been on a pony before. I paid big bucks for that animal and he's being ruined.'

'Who on earth is that?' asked Charles.

'Kelly's dad, Con Lynch. We call him the gorilla.'

'Who's we?'

'Maggie, a good friend of mine. She thought of it.'

'She must be pretty sharp.'

For some reason I felt slightly irritated at his admiring compliment. Maggie sharp? I had never thought of her in that light.

'I think we'll call it a day,' said Mr Frank smoothly. 'They're all getting a bit tired. I've asked a lot of them today. Kelly rarely knocks a fence – and it does happen to the best riders.'

I had to admire Kelly. She sat there coolly, saying not a word. But I could feel she was seething with rage at being talked to like that in front of the Blakes.

'She'll do that fence again,' shouted Mr Lynch. 'And get it right.'

Mr Frank withdrew with a shrug of his shoulders, and for a second I thought the gorilla was about to come into the arena, rebuild the fence and force

Kelly to jump the sequence again.

Mercifully at that moment another voice sounded from beyond the sand-ring and, looking across, I saw Marion Lynch quickly approaching.

'Con, darling,' Mrs Lynch purred as she made her way up to him. 'I need you at the house. Eleanor and the children are staying for lunch. We need your big strong arms to start the gas barbecue so we can cook you up a yummy treat.'

'I'll be there in a minute,' he growled.

'Now!' The voice dripped with icicles.

Con Lynch turned on his heel and retreated toward the patio.

The lunch was certainly yummy and I could see the Blakes tucking in for all they were worth. Mr Frank had excused himself but Con Lynch, now cooled down, hovered about, refilling glasses and plates.

Marion Lynch certainly knew how to handle him.

7 Getting Deeper

The bell rang for the start of class. Miss Maher stopped writing percentage problems on the black-board (tomorrow's homework) and turned to us.

'Good morning, Fifth and Sixth. Hope everyone had a good weekend. Now let's start by checking your homework. All those interesting questions on electricity. How did you get on?'

There was a lot of shuffling of books and rattling of papers – and a few groans – as we all bent down to retrieve our homework from our school-bags. It had been a difficult assignment answering the ten questions on how an electric circuit and switch work. It took me almost an hour to complete and in the end I had to ask Mom for help.

'Miss Maher,' Kelly raised her hand.

'Yes?' Miss Maher looked up. 'What is it?'

Everyone including me looked at Kelly.

'Miss,' Kelly sounded nervous and hesitant. 'I'm terribly sorry. I forgot my homework. I did it, honest, but left it on the desk in my bedroom. You can phone my home and check.'

'That won't be necessary, Kelly,' Miss Maher answered in a kindly voice. 'But you mustn't let it happen again. You're new here so perhaps you don't understand the importance we attach to homework. It's the only way I know you're taking in all I'm teaching you.' She turned to the rest of us. 'What happens to those who forget their homework?'

'We have to stay in at break and do it,' we all chorused.

Miss Maher smiled at Kelly and began to check the rest of the homework.

At eleven, the bell rang for break. Not a moment too soon. I was feeling drained after two tough sessions of decimals and percentages.

'Out you all go and get some air... I think your batteries need recharging. And, remember, all rubbish into the bin. Not on the ground.'

How could you not like Miss Maher? I thought to myself as I grabbed my jacket. She had been so nice and understanding about Kelly. She hadn't even asked her any awkward questions about the homework – which she usually did if she suspected there had been a bit of fibbing involved. She had certainly let her down lightly.

I was in a cheerful mood, glad to know Kelly had done her homework, even if she had forgotten it. I had made a pact with myself over the weekend, never ever to let anyone copy from me again.

I looked up and saw Kelly smiling at me.

'I need to talk to you about something important,' she said, linking my arm and steering me towards a secluded spot near the school wall. 'You've got to lend me your homework for tonight. Or I'll be in serious trouble with that so-and-so.'

'No, Kelly,' I said in a steady voice, 'I'm not going to let you copy from me again. You're only going to get us both into trouble.' I started to walk away from her.

'Clare, you don't understand.' Kelly started to cry. 'Things are terrible at home. My parents had an awful row after the Blakes left on Saturday. Dad threatened to sell Moonstepper because I knocked the gate. Mom said he would do nothing of the sort – just as she was getting friendly with Eleanor Blake and the "horsey set". Dad started roaring and shouting about all the "free-loaders" around Galway. And Mom told him to get out and go back to Dublin if that was what he wanted to do. It was horrible and all because I knocked one lousy fence.'

I didn't know what to say. She had made an honest mistake – we all knocked fences – and now her father was threatening to sell her pony because of it. It made no sense to me at all.

'No one was talking to anyone all weekend. I stayed in my room, couldn't do a thing.'

'But you did your homework,' I said stupidly.

'Oh, that? Of course I didn't. How could I have concentrated on anything? And that hag Maher will have it in for me if I don't have my homework done for tomorrow. I'm useless at that science and maths stuff.'

'But you got all the maths answers last week.'

'Vera helped me. But she won't be at home tonight... please, Clare,' she begged through her tears. 'Just one more time, I promise I'll never ask you again.'

I hated myself for giving in to her for the rest of the

day. But what could I do? Tell Miss Maher? Unthinkable. Or Mom? All she would say was that Kelly Lynch was bad news and I should have known it. Besides I really felt sorry for Kelly. She was my friend. We were competing on a team together. I had to support her in this crisis.

Suddenly I thought of Maggie. I knew she didn't like Kelly but I wouldn't have to mention her name. I'd ask her advice. I hadn't seen much of her during the week but I was sure she'd turn up this Monday after school.

'Anyone seen Maggie O'Connor?' I asked some girls who were talking to Brenda outside the school as they waited for their lift home. Brenda's mother cleaned the school every afternoon so Brenda had to

wait until she was finished.

'She's gone,' said one of the girls.

'Ya, Clare,' crowed Brenda. 'Drove off with the O'Briens a couple of minutes ago.'

I was bewildered. In spite of everything I had really expected Maggie to come home with me.

When Mom finally came to pick up Sam and me, she didn't seem to notice Maggie's absence. She was bubbling over with news of her own.

'Remember when I took that drive after school last week?' she asked excitedly. 'Well, you won't believe it.'

'What, Mom?' asked Sam. 'Win the Lotto or something?'

'No, I didn't win anything. But I certainly learned a lot. It seems that Mattie Stone *did* own River Run's grand-dam some twenty years ago...'

I don't know whether Sam was listening to the litany of names that followed. I certainly wasn't. All I could think about was Maggie. Why hadn't she come home with us as usual? Was she still mad about Kelly and the Blakes and the Saturday practice sessions? Well, if that was the way she felt, good luck to her. I was really annoyed.

'... I wrote to the vet whose name was on the passport. He wrote back today to say that Mattie Stone *did* own the dam of Inis Eagla and he would vouch for the fact she was a pure Irish Draught mare. So you can imagine how excited I am.'

I stifled a yawn.

8 Best Friends

The next morning I awoke to the smell of rashers frying. I looked at my digital clock and saw that it was just after half-past eight. I had asked Mom the night before to wake me up early so that I could ride before school but maybe the weather had turned stormy. I got out of bed and walked over to my bedroom window to check. The sky was overcast but the branches of the trees in the orchard were hardly moving and there were no fresh puddles in the yard. Mom must have just forgotten. I was glad because my whole body ached.

I hadn't slept well. Between Saturday's practice session and Kelly and her homework I had plenty to worry about.

And now it seemed I couldn't even rely on Maggie to talk things over with. I must have tossed and turned all night because when I stared into the small mirror that hung beside my wardrobe, I was surprised to see my hair, that usually fell long and straight, sticking out in all directions. I hadn't the energy to tackle the snarls so I hastily pulled it back in a pigtail and headed downstairs.

'Morning, sleepyhead,' said Mom as I walked into the kitchen and collapsed into the big armchair next to Tiny. She was standing at the counter making sandwiches for our school lunch.

'Dad and I decided to give you a day off from exercising Piggy. You've been at it every morning for the last week.'

'But, Mom,' I insisted. 'He needs the extra work. He's far too fat for the competition.'

'And you're far too pale. Do you feel all right?' Mom dried her hands on a dishcloth and walked over to feel my forehead with the palm of her hand. 'You've no temperature but I've heard there's a bad bout of aches and pains going round.'

'Mom, I'm fine.' I tried to sound convincing. 'Where are Dad and Sam?'

'Feeding the horses. Sit down and eat this rasher sandwich while it's hot. It's almost time to leave for school.'

She held up a plate of toast and rashers and a glass of orange juice. I dragged myself out of the armchair and over to the kitchen table and sat down. It took less strength to eat than to complain.

I spent the entire day at school feeling like I was walking on egg-shells. I watched Miss Maher's face when Kelly handed in her homework for correcting. No reaction. She just put the pile aside for checking later. I was still full sure that later she would call Kelly and me into the staff room and tell us that we were both in trouble – but she didn't.

I thought Maggie, never one for keeping things bottled up, would explode and tell me what a rotten friend I was – but she didn't.

I was positive Kelly would ask me for my

homework during break – but she didn't.

Miss Maher acted normally towards me. Maggie just avoided me. I avoided Kelly.

On Wednesday, everyone in class seemed normal except me. Again, I felt on edge, waiting for something to happen. Every time Kelly or Miss Maher spoke I thought it would be about yesterday's wretched homework. I felt I would have to talk to someone about how I was feeling or I would go mad.

'Listen up, Fifth and Sixth,' Miss Maher began when we came back from lunch-break. 'I have to leave early today to go to a school meeting.' We all cheered.

'And I have some good news and some bad news,' she continued. 'Fifth class will have their usual spelling test.'

Groans from the Fifth. 'So I will ask one of you from Sixth,' she had a quick look around, 'Marie Dooley, to dictate the words.'

'Each student from Fifth will be paired with someone from Sixth who will be responsible for correcting and scoring the test. The sheets will then be collected by Mrs Forde who will be keeping an eye on you from next door. The good news is that when you have finished, she'll put on a video for you.' Cheers replaced the groans.

I wasn't surprised that Kelly and I were paired off as we sat at the same table.

'Clare,' she whispered to me, 'make sure I get the spellings right.'

Marie Dooley walked up to the front of the

classroom and dictated the ten words on her list. Beside me, Kelly wrote hesitantly. She seemed to be struggling. When time was up, she passed her sheet to me. I couldn't believe my eyes. She had mis-spelled every single one!

Word	*Kelly*
plastic	pilastick
children	cheldern
follow	fealo
machine	masaen
service	srve's
missile	misial
salary	salre
fields	fildes
woman	wowne
favourite	vevvort

'You've got to help me,' Kelly pleaded.

I hastily tore a second sheet from Kelly's copy and scribbled down the ten words in handwriting that I tried to make as much like Kelly's as possible. I used three of her mis-spellings and corrected the rest; marked 70% on the top and handed it to Mrs Forde, who had, luckily, started collecting at the other end of the room. Even though I had been careful, under the cover of books, to shield my rewriting I wondered if anyone had noticed.

I thought maybe not. The girls next to us at our table were too busy concentrating on their own task of correcting and I doubted if any of the other tables in the room could have seen me. But I was worried that Miss Maher would notice that the writing was not Kelly's. If she did, she would know that someone else had done Kelly's test for her.

Kelly was all over me after school that day. She linked arms with me, gave me her extra carton of orange juice, and told the other girls we were best friends forever. When Brenda Fahy walked over to us while we were waiting for our lifts home beside the school wall, Kelly ignored her. When she finally got the message and moved away, I glanced over and got a menacing look.

9 Accused

I didn't hear any noise in the kitchen so I slipped quietly down the back stairs, hoping that Mom and Dad were still outside doing the herding. They usually set off on horseback at the first light of day, Mom on River Run, Dad on his big chestnut gelding Casey, to check any stock out on the land, jumping the single stone walls that separated the different fields. Mom loves these early morning rides; when something prevents her from going she is, to quote Dad, 'cross as a bear'. I love going too and Piggy revels in the freedom of an open field as well as the company of stable-mates.

But not today; I just wasn't up to it. Not with that cloud of Kelly and her homework hanging over me. Mom said that if I didn't feel any better by next week she was going to phone the doctor. She already had me taking a horrible-tasting iron tonic.

The familiar sounds of early morning cartoons filtered in from the sitting-room; Sam was taking full advantage of Mom and Dad's absence, and the 'No TV before 6 pm' rule. I sat down at the kitchen table and as I picked up an apple I noticed three horse passports stacked neatly beside the fruit bowl. Half interested, I opened the newest-looking one. Tiny heard the noise from the armchair where he was curled up and lifted his head momentarily to see if food was being offered before returning to his nap.

The passport belonged to River Run, Mom's mare, described as a 16.3-hand grey, born in 1992, out of the dam Inis Eagla and sired by Powerswood Purple (RID #737).

I moved on to the oldest-looking book. This passport belonged to an unnamed bay mare, 15 hands, owned by Martin Stone. Martin Stone? Was that the man Mom was burbling about in the car coming home the other day? The pages were yellowed with age but the print was still legible. It said that the mare was foaled in 1971, by an unrecorded dam sired by Aughadown (RID #565).

The third passport belonged to a 15.3-hand chestnut mare named Inis Eagla, foaled in 1983, out of an unrecorded dam and sired by Ballinrobe Boy (RID #703). This mare was owned by Brendan Dolan from Gort, a town twenty minutes away.

What was it all about? I threw the passports aside and tried to think of what I would say to Miss Maher if she accused me of doing Kelly's spelling test for her.

The school morning was a merciful blank and I began to revive a little. After lunch we filed back into our classroom, the room feeling hot and stuffy after the cold fresh air outside. Miss Maher was standing behind her desk looking bothered. I could feel that something was wrong. I looked around the room searching for a clue. My eyes fell on Kelly who, strangely, had not come back to my table but was sitting at one, two away. Her face was pale and her eyes were red from crying. I hadn't seen her at break

(I had been keeping a sharp eye out for her so that I could avoid a tete-a-tete) but she wasn't in the school yard and I assumed she had been let off early to go somewhere with her mom or dad.

I gave an inward groan. Kelly had been spoken to. Now it was my turn. And mine was the worst crime. It wasn't Kelly's fault she couldn't spell but I had deliberately falsified her test. That was cheating of the first order. I was in for it.

'Fifth and Sixth classes,' Miss Maher began in a serious voice. 'An incident has occurred which will not be tolerated at this school. One of your class-mates has been made fun of in an extremely hurtful way. This is a form of bullying and is totally unacceptable.'

Silence followed. We had all heard stories about bullying. Gangs that picked on little kids or older children who didn't fit in. But it was hard to imagine Kelly Lynch (and it must have been her) in the role of victim. And bullying had never happened at our school before.

'Now, take out your history books and turn to page thirty-five,' said Miss Maher. The sermon was over for the time being.

After school, there was a buzz of gossip and guesswork in the corridor as we collected our coats. Kelly was nowhere to be seen. I asked Bernie Molloy what had happened. She whispered to me that Kelly had found a note stuck between the pages of her homework diary after the morning break and that she heard some other girls had got one too.

What was it? It must have been very hurtful to have Kelly in tears? And who could have sent it? She wasn't that well known yet. We all got caught occasionally sending notes to each other but Miss Maher never got too upset about it. I was sure Kelly would tell me about it later – I was surprised she hadn't told me first. But why had she changed tables? And rushed off in such a hurry?

'Nice friend,' Brenda spat as she brushed past me, shoving me to one side.

'What do you mean?' I asked, regaining my balance and catching up with her.

'Kelly knows it was you,' Brenda sneered. 'You had to tell on her, Miss Goody Two-Shoes.'

'I didn't write any note,' I said hurriedly. 'I don't even know what was in it.'

'And you know what else? Kelly asked if she could change her seat. That's what she thinks of you.' She pushed past me for the second time.

I didn't do anything for what seemed like ages. I was too stunned by what had just occurred. Someone had written a nasty note about Kelly. And Brenda was actually saying that I had written it. But that was crazy! Kelly would never believe that. We were best friends. I had to find her.

I went out and around the building to where everyone was waiting for their lifts home. I saw Maggie talking to the O'Brien girls and Sam trying out a few karate moves with his friends. But where was Kelly? I *had* to find out what had happened. On an instinct I turned back and made my way around to the bicycle shed. Kelly and Brenda were standing there as if they were waiting for me.

'Hi, Kelly,' I said as I approached her. 'I'm glad I found you before you went home.'

'I don't talk to traitors,' said Kelly in a cold voice. 'Go back to Saggie Maggie, if she'll have you.'

'But I didn't do anything, Kelly,' I begged. 'You've got to believe me.'

'Get lost,' Brenda said, linking her arm through Kelly's.

Both girls burst out in a fit of laughter. I turned and walked to the front of the school, body numb, fingers trembling. What was I do to?

Next morning in the school yard, I looked around for someone to talk to but everyone seemed to be turning their backs on me. Brenda must have told them that I had sent the note. I stood by myself until the bell rang.

When I entered the classroom I noticed that everyone had a sheet of paper with something written on it. There was giggling and whispering and a lot of looks directed at me. I slowly picked up the sheet which was left on my chair and felt my legs go weak when I recognised the writing. *Kelly's!* It was a photocopy of an essay that we had been given earlier in the week about the famine. It was full of mis-spellings and cross-outs and the handwriting was terrible.

I saw Brenda pointing at me, then taking Kelly's arm and marching her out through the door. Where

✓

The famine was in the 1840s. many peoples dide as a rult of patowbut and of hangerfevep a nother fever was tetse peses A Lot of pepple went Amerecai Rusia and other contries herped by giveg food to the Irish,

Kelly,
    Good facts but watch your spellings!

Correct:
 died
 result
 potato blight
 typhus
 Russia
 countries
 giving

were they headed? The staff room? Brenda was saying in a carrying voice that most of us could hear, 'Wait till Miss Maher sees this! Clare Fox will really be in trouble this time.'

I managed to sit down. I could feel the others staring. I didn't care. I just wanted to go home.

Then I noticed another piece of paper on my desk, face down. I turned it over. There, in crude capitals, were the words:

KELLY LYNCH IS STUPID.
THAT'S WHY SHE CHEATS

'Are ye listenin'?' A familiar voice rang out above the chatter. Maggie!

'Have ye no brains? Clare Fox no more sent that note or essay than I did. I can swear to it. Now leave her be.'

That was all I could take. I put my head down on my table and began to sob.

10 Struggling

On Saturday morning I awoke with a terrible headache. I had spent the entire night thinking about what had happened. I had come home from school and gone straight upstairs. When Mom followed me up, I told her I felt dizzy and wanted to lie down. When she brought up my dinner an hour or so later, she asked if there was anything wrong. I lied and said no. I still thought if I could only talk to Kelly on her own, she would realise that I was not to blame. I decided to speak to her after the practice session.

A few hours later, our team was lined up in front of Mr Frank in the Lynches' sand-ring. He was looking troubled.

'This just will not do. You must concentrate if you expect to ride well in the competition next Saturday.'

I knew he was talking to me. Kelly, Charles and Charlotte had ridden each of their rounds without a mistake, while I, on the other hand, had two refusals at the spread. What made Piggy do it?

'If you let your ponies gallop heedlessly there is no way you can expect them to jump a fence with precision or make a proper turn back. We'll take a ten-minute break and then try it again.'

Shaking his head, he walked out of the ring.

'Kelly,' I called, turning Piggy out of line and urging him forward past Grey Mist to where she and

Moonstepper stood.

'Can I talk to you for a minute? It's important.'

'Charlotte, do you want a Coke?' Kelly asked, turning to Charlotte who was busy fixing her hair net. 'I have a couple of cans over in the tack room. Come on.' She took her whip and brushed it lightly against Moonstepper's flank, making him leap forward in the direction of the gate. Charlotte, without a word, picked up her reins and trotted after her, leaving me alone in the ring with Charles.

'What's up between you two?' he asked, riding up next to me. 'I thought you were best friends.'

Hobo sniffed noses with Piggy before stretching out his neck to relax.

'What do you mean?' I answered, trying to look totally unconcerned.

'Come on, Clare,' he said gently. 'You've been great up to now on the team. The most consistent of all of us. Something's wrong. Even Mr Frank noticed it – I saw him staring at you in disbelief.'

I looked over at him. He was so different from Charlotte who was totally wrapped up in herself and her image. He really did seem to care about people and their feelings. I could sense that he was trying to help me.

'Kelly thinks I did something to her at school last week,' I explained. 'But I didn't and she won't believe me.' I found it hard to keep my voice steady.

'What does she think you did?'

'She thinks I wrote a nasty note about her. But, honest, I didn't.'

I looked at him again. Would *he* believe me?

'What did the note say?' he asked.

'It said she was so stupid that she had to cheat.'

'But why? And why accuse you?'

'I suppose because she was giving in homework that wasn't hers. It was sometimes mine. And then I told her I wouldn't let her copy mine any more.'

'Kelly's not very academic, is she?' he laughed. 'Did you know she was supposed to start at Mount Inver this term but she never appeared? I wonder was it something to do with...' Charles suddenly stopped. 'Shssh... pretend we weren't speaking. Here come the girls.'

He turned his pony towards the gate and I heard him shout, 'Thanks for the Coke. I know now where I stand in your lives.'

'Right, class.' Mr Frank walked back into the ring. 'Let's make this part of the lesson count. Will you all pick up an ordinary trot going to the right?'

The second half of the practice lesson didn't go much better. No refusals this time. Only a run-out. Only! Mr Frank despised riders who let their ponies run out. 'Who's in charge?' he would say in a withering tone. 'You or your pony?'

But how could I concentrate when my life was falling to pieces all around me? I couldn't believe that Kelly would refuse to talk to me. And just to rub in her dislike she made a big point of inviting the Blakes back to the house for lunch after the practice. Just the Blakes. Not me.

I rode Piggy home, more troubled than ever. I

untacked him, put on his turnout rug and led him out to the front field to roll in the grass and graze in the afternoon sun.

I leaned against the post and rail fence, watching him and thinking about Kelly.

The one bright spot was Maggie. She had stood up for me. But I knew Maggie. She had a great sense of fair play and would have stood up for anyone she thought had been wrongly accused. There was nothing more to it than that. Otherwise she would have waited for me after school.

'How's my girl?'

I felt a strong arm embrace my shoulder. I looked up and saw Dad smiling at me. I knew instinctively

Mom had sent him to find out what was going on. She knew I wasn't any good at keeping secrets from him.

'It's Kelly Lynch, isn't it?' he probed.

I felt a lump forming in my throat. I slowly nodded.

'She's done something to you?'

Again I nodded.

'Is it over the ponies?'

I shook my head, feeling my eyes begin to water.

'It's school then.'

I slowly nodded. I was trying not to cry.

'Do you know your mom and I have been worried sick about you?'

The kindness in his voice was too much. I had to tell him. I produced the note, now crumpled, that I had kept hidden in my pocket, the note that said:

KELLY LYNCH IS STUPID.
THAT'S WHY SHE CHEATS

'This?' He looked bewildered.

'It was left in Kelly's homework. And several other girls got it too. Kelly thinks I wrote it! Everyone does.'

'What does it mean?'

'Dad, I can't tell you just yet… I'm trying to sort it out… please.'

'Well, I'll give you a few days. No longer. We may need to go and see Miss Maher.'

I nodded once again and turned to bury my face in the front of his warm fuzzy jumper.

11 Two Magpies

I slept so late on Sunday morning that I wondered if Mom had slipped something into the hot chocolate she brought me after my talk with Dad. What finally woke me was the sound of a car driving into the yard. I raised myself up on my elbow, just high enough off my bed to see Mom turning the jeep and horse-box around in the yard. She lowered the ramp and a sturdy chestnut mare, heavy in foal, slowly backed out of the box. She neighed excitedly as Mom led her into a stable.

I didn't remember Mom or Dad talking about getting a new brood-mare but maybe I just hadn't been listening. I waited for Mom to reappear before getting out of bed and going to the window. As I opened it, a cold blast of air hit me in the face and chest, making my whole body shiver.

'Mom,' I yelled down at her, 'what mare is that?'

She looked up at me and smiled. Her hair was wet and her anorak and wellingtons were spattered with mud.

'That's Inis Eagla,' she said proudly. 'And she was a right devil to catch!'

'What's she doing here?' I asked, hugging myself tightly in an effort to keep warm.

'Brendan Dolan loaned her to me for the inspection. Come on down and I'll fill you in.' She disappeared into the house.

Inis Eagla? That rang a bell. Where had I seen that name before? Then I remembered. The passport. The third passport I had looked at on the kitchen table. River Run's dam. So Mom was having luck in her search for the three generations of Irish Draught. But what about the oldest passport, the one with the yellowed pages? Had she found the owner?

I felt guilty as I closed the window and hurriedly dressed. I knew I hadn't been exactly sympathetic over the past few days. I just hadn't been interested in her crusade to try and establish River Run's identity as a pure Irish Draught – and, boy, had I made it clear. I decided that just for one day I was going to forget Kelly and Maggie and Brenda and Charlotte – the lot – and show some family solidarity.

Down in the kitchen, I saw, with a pang, my late breakfast all ready and waiting.

'Tell me about Inis Eagla,' I said brightly taking a seat at the kitchen table. 'Black pudding – yum! – two please... Why does she have to be inspected?'

'It's a long story...'

'Mom, I've got all day.'

'Well,' Mom began, taking a seat in the chair across from me. 'In order for River Run to become a registered Irish Draught, I have to prove she has three generations of pure draught breeding. So I've been trying to piece together her family tree. Inis Eagla was the easy part of it. Tracing her grand-dam, who would be dead at this point, was much harder. But Mattie Stone turned up trumps. So, here's what

River Run's pedigree looks like at the moment.' She took a sheet of paper from under the three passports that were still stacked in the middle of the table.

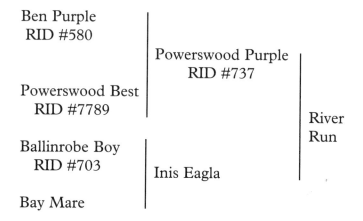

Ben Purple
RID #580

Powerswood Purple
RID #737

Powerswood Best
RID #7789

River
Run

Ballinrobe Boy
RID #703

Inis Eagla

Bay Mare

'So River Run is third generation,' I said positively as I studied the handwritten sheet. 'Now how do you register her?'

'It's not all that easy. There have to be blood tests and an inspection. John Moran is coming today to take blood samples from both River Run and Inis Eagla – that's why I had to collect her this morning. Then, tomorrow, two judges will be travelling over from Dublin to inspect both mares. If the blood tests match up to their recorded dams and sires and the result of the inspection is satisfactory, then I think we're in business and River Run will be registered by the Draught Society as a full Irish Draught.'

'But what does it really mean – at the end of it all?'

'As I told you before – but I don't think you were

listening – River Run will be eligible to compete in all sorts of valuable showing classes against her own kind. And if she has a foal, particularly a filly, it will be worth a great deal of money as a purebred foal. And all the money we make from our prize winnings and future foals will go toward the purchase of the duck-pond field.'

'Oh, Mom, and you did all that work while I was moping about.'

'Not to worry. The Irish Draught Society has been really helpful. But my biggest break, without a doubt, was finding Mattie Stone. I remember a couple of weeks ago stopping by a farm that keeps draught stallions on the far side of the village – Brendan Dolan had told me that Inis Eagla had come from there. When I asked about the mare's history, the owner said he thought she was bred by a man named Stone who lived in Kinvara. When I asked where in Kinvara, he said he thought near an old school, but that Stone was fond of his pints and… I didn't wait to hear; I was off like a shot to Kinvara. Eventually I found where he lived and it was his wife who gave me the bay mare's passport.

'Mattie's only recollection was that on the morning he found Inis Eagla as a newborn foal, two magpies flew overhead and as the saying goes, "one for sorrow – two for joy", he reckoned the foal was bound to bring someone good fortune.'

John Moran arrived after lunch, with a hearty, 'How's the champ?' I liked John. He was always in good humour, always ready to help.

'How's Nick?' I asked him as we followed Mom out to the stables. Nick was his nephew and it was he who had helped me to train Piggy during the summer. Without him, I'd never have won at Ballinasloe. So Nick was really responsible for me being invited to join the team for the Team Hunt Chase.

'He's fine,' replied John opening a small cardboard box that held two test tubes. I recognised the blood-sampling kit, the same kind Dad used when he got John to blood-test his thoroughbred foals. 'Always asking after you and Piggy. Clare, put a head-collar and lead on River Run for your mom. We'll do her first.' Minutes later I had her ready and gave the lead to Mom.

I watched John enter her stable and pat the big mare on the neck as she eyed him worriedly. He talked to her in soothing tones until she relaxed. I watched from outside the stable as Mom continued to talk to her while John withdrew blood from a vein in her neck and filled two different sample tubes with it. He then secured them with rubber stoppers and replaced them in the cardboard box.

'Good job,' he said as Mom removed the head-collar and lead and they both left the stable. ''Ready to do the chestnut mare.'

Mom opened Inis Eagla's door and I watched as the same procedure was carried out.

'I hear Weatherbys is now requiring some mares and foals to be micro-chipped and have hair samples

submitted for DNA testing. Where will it all end?'
Mom asked, giving a deep sigh.

'Progress, Nora, who can stop it?' John said
smilingly as he placed Inis Eagla's blood samples into
a separate cardboard box. 'All set except to fill out
the forms.'

'Great, we'll have a cup of tea while you're at it,'
Mom said leading the way back to the house.

Once the completed forms and the blood-sampling
kits were ready to post, John, Mom, and I relaxed
around the kitchen table drinking mugs of tea and
eating slices of freshly baked apple cake. When Mom
was called outside to deal with a local traveller, John
turned to me.

'Hear you're doing great things – the Team Hunt
Chase – now that's class.'

'I doubt we'll do well,' I said weakly.

'So what. It'll be good fun and great experience. Who's on your team?'

'Kelly Lynch...' He raised his eyebrows but said nothing. '...and Charles and Charlotte Blake – do you know them?'

'Sure. Look after their ponies. Usually out of the good of my heart. They have this aristocratic habit of paying the bills once a year!' He winked at Mom who had returned and was standing at the kitchen door listening.

'Clare likes Charles, I gather,' remarked Mom. 'And doesn't care for Charlotte.'

'Mom,' I gasped, looking at her indignantly.

'Don't worry,' laughed John. 'I'll never tell. Charles is a nice boy. Charlotte is okay if you take no nonsense from her.'

'What's the family like?' Mom asked returning to the table.

'Very, very old,' John said, finishing his mug of tea. 'One of the original "tribes" of Galway. Not much left of that now. Lovely old house. Needs about a million to put it into habitable order. Beats me why they don't turn it into a country hotel or a B&B. They'd get big grants from the government to do it up. But I can't see Mrs B rolling up her sleeves and getting stuck in.'

Nor could I. The thought of her welcoming guests and giving a hand in the kitchen or dining-room was definitely a non-starter.

'Why don't they sell it?' asked Mom.

'They may have to. Unless Charles marries a millionaire.'

'Not very many millionaires around here.'

'You'd be surprised. Look at the Lynches.'

'They're not all that seriously rich, are they?'

'Maybe not yet. But by the time Kelly reaches marriage age, I'd say they'd be in the big league. Property developers are making fortunes.'

Charles and Kelly? I was stunned. It seemed odd to hear people talking so openly about marrying for money. Like old country match-makers.

'Mom,' I said when John had gone. 'If the Lynches are all that rich, why doesn't Mr Lynch just give you and Dad the duck-pond field? It's not worth anything to him.'

She laughed. 'These people didn't get where they are today by giving away duck-pond fields for nothing. But things are looking possible now. Thanks to these.'

She tapped her fingers on the two large brown envelopes containing the blood samples and smiled.

12 Off the Hook

I was watching telly in the sitting-room later that evening when I heard a knock on the front door. Mom was in the kitchen getting supper and Dad was there too, filling in his herd register. I got up slowly to answer it. No one but salesmen or campaigners ever used the front door; everyone we knew always came in through the back.

'Hi, Clare,' a voice greeted me as I opened the door. I was astonished to see Miss Maher standing there smiling at me. 'Are your parents in?'

'Sure,' I managed to say, feeling a knot form in the pit of my stomach. 'They're in the kitchen.' I led the way through the sitting-room.

'Hello, Mr and Mrs Fox,' said Miss Maher. 'Hope I'm not intruding but I was passing by and took a chance I'd find you in.'

'Not at all,' said Mom. 'We'll be having our supper in a little while. Why don't you join us?'

'Thanks, but I can only stay a few minutes.'

'Tea, then?'

'That would be nice.' She sat down at the table across from Dad as Mom filled a mug from the teapot on the range – Dad always seemed to be brewing fresh pots of tea at all hours of the day and night.

I slipped into the armchair next to Tiny. I was

dreading what Miss Maher was about to say.

'Clare,' she said having taken a sip of tea, turning around to look at me, 'I think you know why I'm here. We need to straighten out a few things that have happened very recently at school.'

I nodded and bowed my head.

'You probably know that Kelly Lynch has joined us at St Colman's,' she said to Mom and Dad. They nodded.

Well of course they knew. I must have told them a hundred times.

'There was something different about Kelly from the start. Her reading wasn't fluent – anything but. And she was very erratic about homework. Sometimes it was there. Sometimes she "forgot" it. Sometimes it was absolutely right. Sometimes very wrong. There was just no pattern to it.

'Then there was the famous spelling test. Kelly was scored at seventy per cent by Clare here.'

I blushed at this point. Mom and Dad were looking at me. I knew they, particularly Mom, were bewildered.

'Then last Thursday, Kelly came to see me. Someone had slipped a note into her homework diary, and circulated a few other copies, with the words "Kelly is stupid. That's why she cheats." At first it didn't make sense. Then I thought of the homework. I got out the sheet with the spelling test. Seven right, three wrong. And the handwriting seemed a bit odd. I knew Clare and Kelly sat together. Had Kelly copied from Clare? Or,' she looked at me again, 'did you write them out for her?'

'I wrote them out,' I said miserably.

'But why?' asked Mom.

Miss Maher held up her hand. 'We'll go into that later. But when Kelly handed in her essay on the famine, I knew then what was wrong. Kelly has dyslexia.'

'Is that a disease?' asked Dad.

'No, no,' reassured Miss Maher. 'It is a condition a child is usually born with that can affect the way they learn to read, write or spell. It may cause them to confuse or reverse letters and words as well as directions.'

'Is that why Kelly sometimes gets her left mixed up with her right at our practice sessions?' I asked, feeling a kind of weight lifted off my shoulders for the first time in days.

'Probably. And that's why she is a class behind you at school. I made a phone call to her old school and spoke to the head teacher who said Kelly had great difficulty learning. Had to repeat a class. She put it down to the fact that she didn't take any interest in school work. Poor Kelly! She must have spent most of her school years trying to cover up her learning difficulties. And the only ways she could do it were to stay away from school – or cheat.'

'That must have been hard for her.' Mom sounded sympathetic.

'Very. But dyslexics are usually quite intelligent and learn to cover up brilliantly. Kelly knew that Clare was good at school. So she figured that if she came to St Colman's she could get to copy her homework. She didn't bargain on Clare refusing. Probably thought that because of their common interest in ponies, Clare wouldn't want to lose her friendship.'

'How come Kelly's parents didn't notice all this – the dyslexia, I mean?' queried Mom.

'It *is* strange. But it's unbelievable how often parents don't scent trouble when a child is slow to learn. They often put it down to immaturity or lack of concentration. It *never* occurs to them that there could be a real reason like dyslexia. It's very hard to learn to read if the letters and words are all in a jumble.'

'But who wrote the note about Kelly being stupid?' I asked.

Miss Maher was putting on her jacket, preparing to leave. She gave a bit of a grin. 'I have my suspicions. But I've a few things to check out first.'

'So Clare is off the hook.' It was more of a statement than a question from Dad.

'Of course. Why would she want to upset Kelly? It never made sense. No...it's more likely to be someone who wanted to make Kelly think badly of Clare and drive a wedge between them. A friend of Kelly's or of Clare's... Thanks for the tea, Mrs Fox. See you tomorrow, Clare.'

A minute later Mom and Miss Maher were in the front hall saying good-bye. I leaned back in the armchair and sighed. Dad turned to me and said, 'I bet you're feeling better.'

'Yeah. I think I'll go for a quick ride before supper.'

I slipped out through the back door just in time to see Miss Maher drive away in her small red car. I ran into the stable with Rex close behind me, a new feeling of energy flooding over me. I grabbed a headcollar, a lead and my grooming kit and waltzed down to Piggy's stable.

'Hi, River Run. Hi, chestnut mare. Hi, Casey,' I sang out and as I opened Piggy's door I exclaimed, 'How is the best pony in the entire world?' I threw my arms around him and knew things could only get a whole lot better.

But that night, I lay awake thinking of what Miss Maher had said: 'Someone who wanted to drive a wedge between Kelly and Clare.'

There were only two people to whom that could apply. Brenda – or Maggie. Maggie had made it very clear that she was annoyed with me. Maybe she felt I had done something bad to her. Then I remembered the way she had stood up for me. It just couldn't be Maggie.

I wished it were this day next week. Then the whole wretched thing would be out in the open, or so I hoped.

13 Back on Top

I was looking forward to school on Monday, yet dreading it. Looking forward to it because Miss Maher would probably tell everyone I wasn't the culprit. Dreading it in case she named Maggie.

I didn't have long to wait.

When Fifth and Sixth were assembled Miss Maher, looking unusually grave, asked for everyone's attention.

'Last Thursday, as you all know, something happened which I hope we'll never see again in this school. An anonymous note accusing Kelly Lynch of being stupid and a cheat was circulated. And Clare Fox was accused of writing it. Then on Friday copies of an essay by Kelly, something which should have only been seen by me, were given to everyone in the class. It was meant to hold Kelly up to ridicule in a mean and cruel way. And it was clearly designed to make Kelly mistrust Clare.

'I can now declare that Clare Fox did not write that note. Nor did she send around copies of Kelly's essay. I hope...' this with a wry smile, 'that this will be a lesson to all of you not to jump to conclusions so hastily. School is supposed to make you think for yourselves. So, in future, think. You're not sheep.'

'Please, Miss.' A hand shot up. 'Who *did* write the note?'

It was Maggie speaking! My heart leaped. So Maggie couldn't have sent the note; otherwise she wouldn't have asked.

'That, as they say, is a very good question. At first I was undecided whether to reveal the name or not. I finally decided I had to. If I didn't, everyone would be under suspicion. I spoke to this girl yesterday. She isn't in class today.'

Everyone looked at everyone else. I did a quick scan: Maggie, Kelly, Ciara, Susan, Aine, Orla... Then my eye fell on a vacant chair at the table where Kelly was sitting. I knew it well, from the evil glances that used to be directed at me when Kelly was at my table. Brenda! Brenda Fahy! So it *was* her.

'I know you've all guessed it,' said Miss Maher who was already opening a textbook. 'All I ask you is not to judge her too harshly. She was under a lot of pressure, not of her own making. So – I rely on you all to forget the incident and hold out the hand of friendship... Now, copy down this Irish poem.'

Kelly rushed after me when we went out for break.

'Clare,' she said in a coaxing voice, 'I want to apologise. I knew you wouldn't do a thing like that. But I was upset... and Brenda persuaded me. So say you forgive me.'

'Of course,' I said.

Kelly being so friendly to me! Asking for my forgiveness. It was an outcome I'd never have believed possible last Friday or Saturday. And if I had a fleeting thought that Kelly shouldn't have been so quick to believe Brenda, I banished it at once. I had been quick enough to suspect Maggie, even though I knew in my heart of hearts it couldn't have been her. Maybe Kelly had just such a feeling.

But the day was not over yet. Miss Maher asked Maggie and me to meet her in the staff room at half past two.

'You know, of course,' she began briskly, 'that it was Brenda Fahy.'

'But why?' I asked. I still found it hard to believe that Brenda was the culprit. She had been Kelly's faithful sidekick long before Kelly came to St Colman's. It didn't make sense she would expose her to ridicule.

'She didn't realise Kelly had, or has, dyslexia – I doubt if she has even heard of it. But she knew Kelly was copying homework. First from you, later from her. Probably nothing would have come of it if Kelly hadn't become so friendly with you.'

'But she wasn't really.'

'Well, Brenda thought she was. Same thing. She thought that if she accused Kelly of being stupid and a cheat, suggesting you were to blame, that she'd get her own back on Kelly and make Kelly distrust you.'

'Did ye say something about pressure?' put in Maggie.

'Family problems,' said Miss Maher. 'I gather Mr Fahy comes and goes and lately he seems to be going for longer times. You know Mrs Fahy works here as a cleaner?'

We both nodded.

'I suspect Brenda was upset when Kelly came here

to school. I don't think she told Kelly her mother was the cleaner. That made her feel inferior. Shouldn't – but that's the way it often is. Never be ashamed of what your parents do... Now, that's enough lecturing for one day. Your lift will be here in a minute, girls.'

'Just one other thing,' I begged. 'How did you find out so quickly?'

'The copying machine. Brenda used to stay behind to wait for her mother. That gave her a chance to use the machine and rifle through my desk for material – such as essays. I checked around. Very few families have copying machines. Except the Lynches, and I doubt Kelly would bother to figure out how to use it!'

So the day ended with a laugh.

We had such a feast of roast chicken, creamed potatoes and stuffing when we got home that day that Dad joked, 'We'll have to have a crisis every week – it inspires Mom.'

'Well, don't expect a repeat performance to-morrow.' said Mom. 'The judges will be here at half past three.'

'Will they give ye "the thumbs up"?' asked Maggie accepting another piece of apple crumble and ice cream. I had explained something about the importance of the inspection to her on the way home from school.

'I don't know what the procedure is. Maybe they give the verdict on the spot. Maybe they go away and send a letter in a few days' time after the blood-typing is complete. That would be absolute agony.'

'Are you going to give them tea afterwards?' asked Dad.

'If they'll stay. Maybe judges don't.'

'I know what ye're on about, Mr F,' grinned Maggie. (She and Dad seemed to have built up a special relationship; had the 'Let's go to Supermac's club' really gotten off the ground?) 'Ye're looking for some freshly baked scones topped with cream and jam.'

'How did you guess? I hope the judges don't gobble up everything.'

After we washed up, Maggie and I went up to my room to chew over the day's events.

'Only thing that gits me,' grumbled Maggie after we had been through the whole thing up and down and inside out, 'is Brenda. She's goin' to be a right stone around our necks from now on.'

'I do feel sorry for her though,' I said. 'I never realised she had such a dreadful home life.'

'The trouble with Brenda,' said Maggie, 'is that she's a born trouble-maker. I don't think she wants to be friendly with us. She's one of those types who'd rather have enemies than friends. Remember how she'd glare at ye, just waitin' for ye to mess up when ye'd be doin' the figure-of-eight on Piggy?'

'I do remember. But maybe if we were more friendly towards her, she'd stop feeling she had to hit out and hurt us. I'm going to try anyway. Don't forget we promised Miss Maher.'

Maggie rolled her eyes. 'I'll try. But she'd better change pretty darn quick. We can't waste the whole year reformin' her.'

For some reason, this made us fall about laughing.

'Coming over tomorrow?' I said as she was leaving.

'Sure, I'll make the tea for all of ye.'

'I think Mom has made a chocolate Swiss roll... and, Mags...' I knew this was going to be hard to say. 'I'm sorry about...everything. You must have thought me pretty awful. Getting so wrapped up in Kelly and the Team Chase. It's not as important as all that.'

'Of course it is. Anyway not to worry.' Maggie gave me a push that nearly knocked me sideways. 'But I'm glad we're best friends again. Missed the cookin'!'

'What about the O'Briens?'

'The O'Briens? Clare, ye've only got to be jokin'. They're nice enough, but dull as ditchwater. Seriously grey, if ye git me. And not a joke between the two of 'em.'

I took Piggy out later that evening. Oh, what a wonderful day.

14 The Inspection

'Please walk the grey mare up to the end of the yard and trot back,' one of the men asked me crisply. It was Tuesday afternoon and the judges had been at the farm for over an hour inspecting River Run and Inis Eagla.

The two men, both older than Dad, wore top-coats and tweed caps and held printed forms on clipboards that they kept writing on. I would have loved to have known what they were saying.

The judges had already examined each mare's passport to check that colour, age, and markings were recorded correctly. They had looked at their conformation, assessing them from every side and angle. Then they had them turned loose in the sand-ring so that they could watch them move freely at a walk, trot, and canter. And now, at last, the final test – the in-hand inspection.

I glanced over at Mom who was standing beside Inis Eagla on the far side of the yard. She looked concerned.

When she saw me looking over she tried her best to smile and gave me a nod of encouragement. I took a deep breath and positioned myself an arm's length from River Run's powerful left shoulder. I would have much preferred leading up Inis Eagla, who was smaller, but Mom had said she could be a bit hard to handle and to leave her to her..

I adjusted my grip on the reins of River Run's bridle before making a clicking sound with my tongue that sent her forward into a lively walk. I stepped out quickly to stay beside her and concentrated on keeping her moving in a straight line. I must have done this in-hand display with Piggy at least a hundred times before but never with a mare this size. She practically lifted me off the ground with every step she took.

As instructed, I walked her to the far end of the yard just as I had seen Mom do with Inis Eagla minutes earlier. Then I turned to the right, keeping her on my inside, and only after we completed the turn did I make another clicking sound urging her to trot. I did my best to keep her straight as I passed by the judges.

I was out of breath when I managed to slow her back to a walk and return to our original spot.

'Thank you,' one of the men said while the other nodded. 'I think that about wraps it up for today.'

They both entered more comments on their forms. When they had finished, they walked back to the car parked beside the house and sat into it. I could see them talking and looking over the printed sheets.

Mom walked over from the far side of the yard leading Inis Eagla. She now looked worried as well as concerned. Passing this Irish Draught inspection meant so much to her. I knew that she had spent the whole morning getting the mares ready, washing their legs and tails, plaiting their manes and tails, and

brushing their coats until they gleamed. But there was nothing more she could do now except to wait for the judges' decision.

'You'll have a cup of tea before you go,' she asked politely when they walked back from the car. 'You must be frozen standing outside for so long.'

I had been so preoccupied with the inspection that I hadn't felt the cold; it was only now that I realised my fingers and toes were numb.

'That would be nice – especially when we have something to celebrate,' one of the judges said warmly, smiling for the first time since he arrived.

'Did you say "celebrate"?' Mom spluttered. 'Did they pass? Are you sure?'

'Quite sure, Mrs Fox,' said the other judge. 'River

Run and Inis Eagla have both passed the inspection with flying colours. They are a credit to the Irish Draught breed. We will take their passports back to Dublin and if the blood-typing matches up when they are returned in the post, River Run will have an RID number printed after her name.'

'I can't believe it,' Mom gasped, shaking both men's hands at the same time. 'Thank you so much. This means more than you'll ever know.'

She turned to me. 'Clare, will you take Inis Eagla so that we can go in and have a cup of tea? I'll send Maggie out to help you.'

I watched the judges follow Mom into the house. A minute later Maggie appeared from around the front of the house eating a buttered scone.

'Did ye see me watchin' from the back window?' she managed to say between bites and swallows. 'I lighted a special candle for ye, a little help from the man upstairs.' She pointed towards the sky and gave a wink.

'Thanks, Mags,' I replied. 'You take Inis Eagla here, and we'll put her and River Run back into their stables and give them a bit of hay. They must be cold and hungry after standing around for so long.'

'Right, boss!' Maggie said exploding into a fit of giggles. It was good to hear her laugh again. As we led the two mares back into the stables, I thought about how much I had missed my best friend.

I got a surprise phone call late on Tuesday evening. Kelly! There was to be a final practice with Mr Frank the following afternoon. Charles and Charlotte had got a half-day off from Mount Inver.

The session went like a dream. Kelly didn't mix up her 'lefts' and 'rights', Piggy didn't refuse or run-out, and Hobo actually put on such a finishing spurt that I could see Mr Frank visibly relax; it looked like his 'team strategy' of a fast finisher could become a reality.

Charlotte and Grey Mist? They performed as usual. No ups, no downs, always in control. I thought of Maggie's 'seriously grey'.

Mrs Lynch invited us into the conservatory afterwards for tea. Wafer-thin cucumber sandwiches. Mushrooms in bite-size pastry cases. Tiny eclairs and the Lobster Pot chocolate cake. All beautifully presented on silver trays lined with lace doilies served by a maid in a frilly apron.

'Just a little something,' twittered Mrs Lynch. 'Didn't want to spoil your appetites for dinner.'

Judging by the way Charlotte and Charles tucked in, Mount Inver's dinner menu didn't seem to promise much to look forward to.

Afterwards, when the Blakes were saying goodbye, Kelly asked me to stay behind. I was flattered. Maybe, after all, Kelly did consider me a best friend.

Upstairs in a bedroom-to-die-for she showed me several items of clothing laid out on the bed. Dark navy and red. I noted navy corduroy trousers, several navy wool skirts, a red and navy striped tie...

'Guess what?' she said. 'These are all for Mount Inver. I'm going there. Starting next week.'

'Mount Inver? But I thought you were staying the year at St Colman's.'

The momentary vision of rides through the late autumn countryside on Moonstepper and Piggy, and practice sessions for next year's competitions suddenly vanished. I felt chilled.

'Funny thing. That nasty Brenda thought she would make me look like a right fool. She did me a great favour. That dyslexia thing. Miss Maher came to see my parents and explained what my problem was. She said I'd need special tuition. That was really why I didn't go to Mount Inver last year with Charlotte and Charles. I failed the entrance. Dad blew up. Can you imagine? Put it about that he and Mum didn't think the teaching was good enough, that I needed a year or two at a national school. Said he'd learned all he knew at a local school.'

'What about the special tuition?'

'Yeah. A lady will give me lessons twice a week.'

'Couldn't you have had them here? And still gone to St Colman's? You said your father wanted you to have a national school grounding.'

'What do you think?' she giggled. 'He and Mum are over the moon that I'm going to Mount Inver. Mum was horrified I had to go to an ordinary national school. I mean, the girls there are a pretty crummy lot. People like Brenda Fahy. Thank God, I never need to see her again.'

What did she see in my face that made her add hastily, 'Not you, of course. You were the only nice thing about St Colman's. I wish you were coming with me. We'd be a great twosome... What do you think of this?' She held up a navy blazer with gold buttons and a school crest sewn on the top pocket. 'We wear this for concerts and special outings...'

On the way home I thought of Maggie. Reliable, dependable Maggie. How could I have been so stupid? Even after Kelly had shown me I was only a stopgap, I was still prepared to come running at the drop of a hat. Well, from now on, I'd be much smarter about people.

Over cold meat and salad – I was starving as I had actually had only one cucumber sandwich and a sliver of cake – I listened to Mom's excited plans for putting River Run in foal and showing her next summer to get the money that would help us buy the duck-pond field.

I didn't mention Kelly.

15 The Team Hunt Chase

Saturday, the day of the Team Hunt Chase, came and went without incident. Our team came in a respectable second. Mr Frank was delighted with us, especially as we were placed ahead of a rival team from one of the big equestrian centres in Galway.

We probably would have won the competition if Charlotte hadn't had a run-out at the chute. When she came off the bank after the turn she lost control of Grey Mist and he bolted over the next small fence and just kept going. Charlotte hadn't time to slow him up to make the turn for the narrow chute and the team lost valuable seconds waiting for her to try again. Charles and I both tried in vain to make up time on our rounds but I never claimed to be a bold rider and Hobo never looked like a racehorse.

Mrs Lynch would have to wait until next year to get a crystal rose bowl for her china cabinet.

The team were to celebrate by going over to the Blakes for a 'pick-me-up' supper, as Mrs Blake called it, with a few other people. I was to call over to Kelly at six o'clock and get a lift to the Blakes with her parents, who were also invited as the team's sponsors. Mr Frank cried off – prior engagement.

I hadn't wanted to go but Mom and Dad urged me.

'Never pass up an experience,' said Dad.

'I'm dying to hear about the house,' added Mom. 'I believe it's beautiful.'

So I went. I decided that if I didn't Kelly would think I was annoyed by her remarks about St Colman's. Besides I was curious.

'Why the blazes do I let you drag me to these sessions?' Con Lynch growled as the four of us drove along a back road signposted for Tuam. 'Slices of watery ham, a bowl of rabbit food, cheap vino; five-star rubbish, that's what we'll get, I bet you.'

'Now, Connie,' cooed Marion Lynch as she peered at her reflection in the small mirror attached to the sun-visor of the passenger side of the car and fussed with a head that didn't have a hair out of place. 'Don't talk like that. The Blakes are worth knowing. Did you know they're related to Lord and Lady Laverton? Eleanor said something about a coffee morning being held at their place next week. That should be fun.'

'Blakes, fakes,' snorted Mr Lynch. 'I'm telling you there's nothing there for us. I don't see them having the dosh to put down on new construction.'

'Con, how often do I have to tell you money isn't everything? These people have connections. They're on the boards of banks and big companies. They know everyone who's worth knowing – and they have land.'

I glanced over at Kelly to see her reaction to this conversation but her eyes were focused on the passing countryside. She wore such a bored expression I decided not to bother her.

Marion Lynch only came to life again when we passed a small school. 'Now take the next left, then the first right, and then the avenue is first on the right,' she directed, reading from a small bit of paper she produced from her snake-skin handbag.

The shock-absorbers on the Lynches' Merc were put to the test as we made our way up a narrow laneway strewn with pot-holes and overgrown whitethorn bushes. At the end of the 'avenue' stood a grey two-storey house with steps up to the front door and bay windows on either side. The Blakes' old BMW was parked outside.

'Blasted holes, blasted briars,' fumed Mr Lynch. 'Too flipping mean to pay for someone to fix the road and trim back the hedges.'

'Here we are,' said Mrs Lynch enthusiastically.

'Look, there's Eleanor waiting for us outside.'

She waved back, Kelly came to life. The gorilla said something under his breath.

As it turned out Mr Lynch was spared the supper of watery ham and acres of lettuce. Eleanor had a tale of woe.

'When we came back from the Hunt Chase, Mary told me cook had been called away unexpectedly – a death in the family, I believe. So instead of the wonderful supper I'd planned I'm going to have to take you to O'Flahertys,' mentioning a small B&B in the nearby village. 'I believe they do wonderful suppers, so it shouldn't be too bad.'

Two 'wonderfuls'. No supper. I had to turn away to hide a smile.

'What a tragedy!' gushed Mrs Lynch. 'I mean for the cook. But we can't let you take us out. We'll go to the Lobster Pot. Con, will you phone them and reserve? How many people?'

'Just you four and us three,' said Eleanor, leading the way into the house. 'I'll pick up the tab, of course. Now don't argue with me. The phone is just here... now, who's for a drink before we set out?'

I wondered what had happened to the other guests.

The drawing-room, with tall elegant bay windows must have been beautiful once. But the walls were dingy and badly in need of a lick of paint, the carpet was frayed and the chair and couch covers rather 'dashed', as Mom used to say.

'Impossible to keep a house when you have dogs,' sighed Eleanor, removing a huge wolfhound from the couch. She took out glasses from a cabinet decorated with gold-coloured birds and scrolls – I could see Mrs Lynch eyeing it. On the walls on either side two bare patches of unfaded wallpaper showed where paintings had once hung.

Mr Lynch came back to say all was well and accept a glass of dark brown sherry.

'Charles, you look after the girls,' called Eleanor. So we gathered at one end of the room and sipped Cokes while Marion and Eleanor discussed antiques at the other.

'You've heard Kelly is coming to Mount Inver?' asked Charles.

'Yes.'

'Very sudden, wasn't it?' said Charlotte.

'Not really,' explained Kelly. 'Dad had this thing about national schools and getting a good grounding there. Then he went off the idea.'

'I'm sorry you're not coming,' said Charles to me. It was what Kelly had said. Only – I felt he meant it. 'Pity the Hunt Chase is over. But we must get together at mid-term and Christmas. Organise an event of our own.'

'That would be great,' I said. 'I'll look forward to it.'

Dinner at the Lobster Pot was as good as the last time. Charles came and sat beside me. This time I didn't bother to see how Kelly was reacting. I don't think she was; she was too busy comparing notes

with Charlotte about her new school.

'The girls at Mount Inver are allowed to wear navy corduroys from Hallowe'en break until the start of spring term,' Clare heard Charlotte explaining. 'Mummy's sister in Boston sent me a gorgeous pair from The Gap.'

'Got to get the priorities straight,' laughed Charles. 'Clothes first, learning last.'

I didn't see any tab being presented.

16 Growing Pains

Maggie came over on Sunday to hear all about the Team Hunt Chase. She was suitably goggle-eyed at the news of Kelly's departure and envious of my second Lobster Pot dinner.

'It wasn't half as much fun as the last time,' I told her. 'I missed you and Nick.'

'What about Charles?' she teased.

'What about him?' I hedged.

'Cripes, look at the time. Got to go. My cousin will be down with her new baby. See ye tomorrow.' She vanished.

'What a funny, mixed-up few weeks it's been,' I said to Mom when we were alone. I was sitting in the old armchair with Tiny in my lap. I could hear the sound of Dad's tractor in the yard and the shouts from the orchard of Sam and his hurling friend. A mouth-watering smell of roast lamb filled the air.

'Well it ended successfully, didn't it?' Mom's voice had a query.

'Very… remember this time last week. It was just before Miss Maher came to visit. I was in a bottomless pit.'

'And I was on tenterhooks about River Run. Now both problems are solved. So all's well that ends well.'

'Not quite.' I had to talk about Kelly. 'I was

disappointed in Kelly. I thought she was a nicer person, that she really liked me.'

Mom shrugged. *'Ni mar a siltear, a bitear.'* Seeing my look of amazement, she laughed. 'Just came to me.'

'What does it mean?'

Translates as "It's not what you think it is."'

'Meaning exactly?'

'Kelly may not be the girl you think she is – and you can take that either way.'

'Meaning Kelly is nicer than I think she is…or not so nice?'

'Exactly.'

Some proverb!

'Then there's Brenda.' I went on. 'All the trouble she caused. But it was a bad time for all of us. Everything seemed to be at sixes and sevens. Me trying to latch on to Kelly. Kelly with dyslexia and having to cheat. Brenda with a broken home. Maggie feeling I'd deserted her. Nothing but problems. Is it always going to be like this?'

'It's worse when you're young – take it from me. In our day we used to call it "growing pains".'

'Growing pains?'

'Yes. It's a medical term. I looked it up once in a dictionary. It means "neuralgic pains in the limbs of the young". When you're growing fast I suppose your bones and limbs are all fighting against each other… to say nothing of your feelings. Now I suppose it would be called something short and snappy.' She paused and added, 'Like PANES – Pre Adolescent

Nervous Energy Syndrome.'

'That about sums it up,' I said darkly. 'Pure pain.'

'But something good did come out of it.'

'How?'

'Kelly will be treated for her dyslexia. Brenda will hopefully make some friends. Maggie has got her best friend back. You've learned a lesson about life... and you've met Charles.'

'I'll never hear from him again.'

'Want to bet.'

'I must say if I lived in that house I'd paint it, fill in the pot-holes and trim the hedges. It could be such a beautiful house. How can they bear to live in it as it is?'

'Probably never notice... say, didn't Charles once say you were very competent? Maybe he'll ask you over, for a house trim and polish.'

Now *I* said, 'Want to bet?'

I almost forgot to mention something else good that came out of those traumatic few weeks.

When I got up to my room that night, there, laid out on the bed, was – a brand-new riding jacket. Just like Kelly's!

Glossary

Colour of a Pony is determined by his coat and his 'points' which include his muzzle, tips of the ears, mane, tail, and legs.

Bay a pony with a dark-brown to bright reddish coat with 'black points'.

Chestnut a pony with a gold to reddish-brown coat with 'similar points'.

Dun a pony with a mouse to yellow colour coat with 'black points'.

Grey a pony with a coat of black and white hairs with 'similar points', the white hairs increasing with age.

Heavy in Foal: a term used to describe a mare that is well-advanced in her eleven-month pregnancy.

Run-out

Refusal: when a pony stops in front of an obstacle which is to be jumped. In show-jumping, ponies are allowed three refusals in each round before elimination.

Run-out: when a pony avoids an obstacle which is to be jumped by running to one side or the other of it.

Shy: when a pony swerves away suddenly in fear from an obstacle or sound.

Refusal

Shy

A Word About Dyslexia

What is Dyslexia?

Dyslexia is a condition that a child is born with that can affect the way he or she learns to read, write, or spell. Dyslexia is not a disease. The condition results from a difference in the structure and function of the brain. Dyslexics tend to have average to above-average intelligence and need to be taught using a structured language programme.

A Child with Dyslexia may:
- have delayed or imperfect speech
- tend to be left-handed or ambidextrous
- have difficulty learning and remembering printed words
- tend to reverse letters or sequences of letters in words (b/d, p/q, n/u, on/no, from/form)
- have persistent spelling errors
- have cramped or illegible handwriting
- have confusion with direction (left/right, up/down)
- have family members with similar problem

For more information contact the:
Dyslexia Association of Ireland, 1 Suffolk Street, Dublin, 2.
Telephone: (01) 6790276

Tack

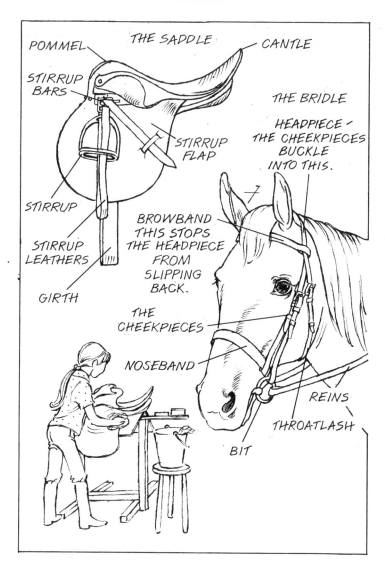

POMMEL

THE SADDLE

CANTLE

STIRRUP BARS

THE BRIDLE

HEADPIECE - THE CHEEKPIECES BUCKLE INTO THIS.

STIRRUP FLAP

STIRRUP

BROWBAND THIS STOPS THE HEADPIECE FROM SLIPPING BACK.

STIRRUP LEATHERS

GIRTH

THE CHEEKPIECES

NOSEBAND

REINS

THROATLASH

BIT